My Furry Foster Family

Tiki the Cockatoo

by Debbi Michiko Florence

illustrated by Melanie Demmer

raintree

a Capstone company — publishers for children

With gratitude, to my editor, Jill Kalz – DMF

Raintree is an imprint of Capstone Global Library Limited, a company incorporated in England and Wales having its registered office at 264 Banbury Road, Oxford, OX2 7DY – Registered company number: 6695582

www.raintree.co.uk
myorders@raintree.co.uk

Text © Capstone Global Library Limited 2021
The moral rights of the proprietor have been asserted.

Edited by Jill Kalz
Designed by Lori Bye
Original illustrations © Capstone Global Library Limited 2021
Production by Tori Abraham
Originated by Capstone Global Library Ltd

Image credits
Capstone Studio: Karon Dubke, 66; Mari Bolte, 69; Melanie Demmer, 71; Roy Thomas, 70

978 1 3982 0463 8

British Library Cataloguing in Publication Data
A full catalogue record for this book is available from the British Library.

Printed in the United Kingdom

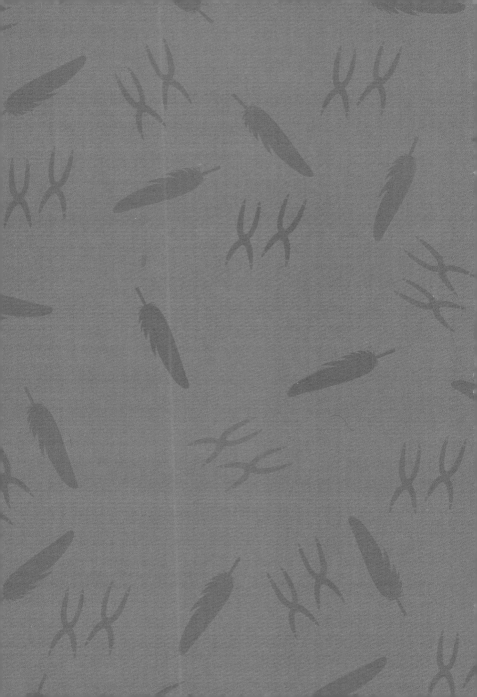

Contents

Dad
(Tim Takano)

Mum
(Cindy Takano)

Me
(Kaita Takano)

Eraser

Ollie

Hannah Miller,
my best friend

Joss Lawrence,
Happy Tails
Rescue

CHAPTER 1

A new cockatoo

I sat down on the sofa next to Mum. Her laptop was open. She was watching videos of parrots.

Yip! Yip! Yip! Ollie, our mini dachshund, pawed my leg. I picked him up. He wanted to watch the parrots too.

We were watching videos of Moluccan cockatoos. They are a type of parrot. Moluccan cockatoos have fluffy, light-pink feathers. When excited, the birds raise the long feathers on their heads.

"I'm happy we're getting a cockatoo to foster," I said.

Mum smiled. "Me too, Kaita," she said. "They are very special birds."

My family fosters homeless animals from Happy Tails Rescue. Mum, Dad and I look after animals until they find their forever homes. Sometimes we adopt the foster animal ourselves.

Happy Tails Rescue helps mostly dogs and cats. But they also help homeless rabbits, snakes and even horses! The Parrot Palace is a special rescue just for parrots. They asked Happy Tails for a foster family for one of their birds. They wanted a family who had spent time with parrots before. Happy Tails called us!

I had never had a bird before. Neither had Dad. But when Mum was little, she had an uncle who had parrots. She helped him look after them nearly every day. Now we were getting a cockatoo called Tiki to foster!

The picture we got of Tiki didn't look like the cockatoos in the videos. Tiki didn't have fluffy pink feathers. In fact, she had no feathers on her chest at all. The skin on her chest was dry and grey. She did have feathers on the rest of her body and her head, though.

"Why does Tiki have feathers missing?" I asked. "Did they fall out? Is Tiki sick?"

"Poor thing," Mum said. "Cockatoos need lots of attention. Tiki's owner didn't spend enough time with her. Sometimes cockatoos pull out their feathers if they get bored or sad."

I hugged Ollie. I love spending time with all of our animals.

Mum shut down her computer. "The good news is, the Parrot Palace rescued Tiki," she said. "They took care of her. After many, many months, she is much better. Her feathers are growing back."

"And now we get to foster her," I said. "I can't wait to find Tiki a forever home!"

Dad walked into the living room. "OK, I think we are ready," he said. "I moved the table out of the spare room. Joss said Tiki's cage is very big and needs a lot of space."

Joss works at Happy Tails Rescue. She is the one who brings us animals to foster. She fostered Ollie before we adopted him!

Yip! Yip! Yip! Ollie stared out of the front window. He wagged his tail.

"Yay! Joss is here!" I said.

Dad took Ollie and put him in my room. We always do that when we get a new foster pet. Ollie is a good foster brother. But he can get too excited sometimes. It's important that the new animals get used to us slowly.

I ran to the door and opened it before Joss rang the doorbell.

"Hi, Joss! We are ready for Tiki!" I said. My breath came out like I had just run down the street.

"Hello, Kaita," Joss said. "I'm glad you're so excited!"

Joss didn't have a box or cage in her hands. I didn't see a bird. I didn't even see a single feather! I peeked behind Joss and looked at her truck.

"Where is Tiki?" I asked.

Joss smiled. "Don't worry," she said. "Tiki is in a pet carrier inside my truck. It's a cool day, so she will be OK until we set up her cage. I need your mum and dad to help me."

I followed my parents and Joss to the truck. In the back was a huge, black, iron cage. It was taller than me! It looked heavy. No wonder Joss needed help.

Joss, Mum and Dad moved the cage slowly up the driveway and into our house. Luckily the cage was on wheels! They rolled it into the corner of the spare room, next to the sofa bed.

Inside the cage was a long perch made out of a tree branch. Food and water dishes were clipped to one side of the cage. On the top of the cage was another long perch. It looked all chewed up.

Joss went back out to the truck to get Tiki. I did a little happy dance. I couldn't wait to meet our new cockatoo!

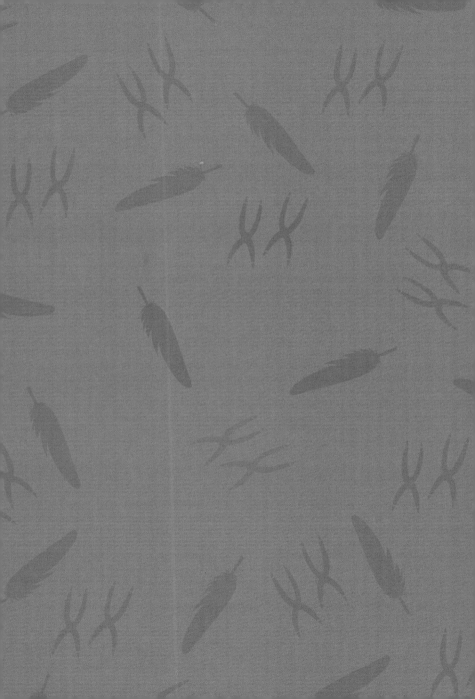

CHAPTER 2

Hello, Tiki!

Joss came back into the spare room with the pet carrier. "Ready, Kaita?" she asked.

"Ready!" I said.

Joss opened the carrier. She held it up to the cage. Tiki came out head first. She hooked her beak on a bar of the cage. The rest of her body and feet followed. She was covered with light-pink feathers.

"Oh! Her feathers have grown back," I said with a grin. "She was missing some in the photo you sent us."

"Yes," Joss said. "It took a while, but Tiki is happier now. She has just one little patch of feathers left to grow."

Tiki climbed to the top of her cage. She stood on the perch.

Mum slowly moved her hand over to Tiki. The bird climbed onto Mum's hand. Mum wrapped her fingers lightly around Tiki's feet.

"Can I hold her?" I asked in a whisper.

"Sure, Kaita," Joss said. "Tiki is a sweet, gentle bird. But, to be safe, please handle her only with your mum or dad around."

"Does that mean I can't come into the room without them?" I asked. That made me sad. I wanted to get to know Tiki on my own.

"Of course not," Joss said. She put her hand on my shoulder. "We want you to spend lots of time with her. She needs love and attention."

"Put out your arm, Kaita," Mum said. "Hold it steady. Tiki will reach out with her beak first, so don't be surprised."

I held out my arm. Tiki reached her beak towards it. She didn't bite. Then she stepped onto me! Tiki gripped my arm with her feet. They felt warm.

I giggled. "Look at me! I'm a tree!" I said. "Hello, Tiki."

Tiki blinked at me. I think that was her way of saying hello.

"Let's get her into her new home," Joss said. She took Tiki and put her into the cage. She filled one of Tiki's bowls with water. She filled the other with special parrot food.

After Joss left, Mum, Dad and I sat down for dinner. Ollie kept peeking into the hallway, towards the spare room.

I laughed. "Ollie has never seen a cockatoo before," I said. "Don't worry, Ollie. Tiki is a big bird, but she's really sweet."

I couldn't wait to spend more time with our new foster pet. Joss said to give Tiki some alone time, though. I would try not to bother her straight away.

After dinner, Mum, Dad and I sat down in the living room. Mum put Ollie on her lap. Dad turned on the TV and started watching a film.

SQUAWK! SQUAAAWK!

We all jumped.

"What was that?" I asked. It wasn't coming from the TV.

Ollie whined and tucked his head under Mum's arm.

AWWWWK!

Another screech hit my ears.

Mum laughed. "That's Tiki!"

"Tiki is making that horrible sound?" Dad asked.

Mum's mouth moved, but I couldn't hear anything she said. Tiki squawked at the same time.

SQUAAAWK!

"What did you say?" Dad yelled to Mum.

"Cockatoos can be very LOUD!" Mum shouted.

I got up and went to the spare room.

AWWWWK!

Tiki clung to the side of her cage.

"I think she's lonely," Mum said, from behind me.

"Can I skip the film?" I asked. "I want to sit in here with her."

Tiki stopped squawking. She cocked her head at me.

"I think she likes the sound of your voice," Mum said.

Mum's words made me happy. She and Dad went back to watch the film with Ollie. I sat on the sofa bed next to Tiki's cage. Tiki watched me quietly.

After a few minutes, I got my sketchbook and started to draw her. I like to draw pictures of all of our foster pets.

Tiki stayed quiet. She ate her food. I sat with her and drew until bedtime.

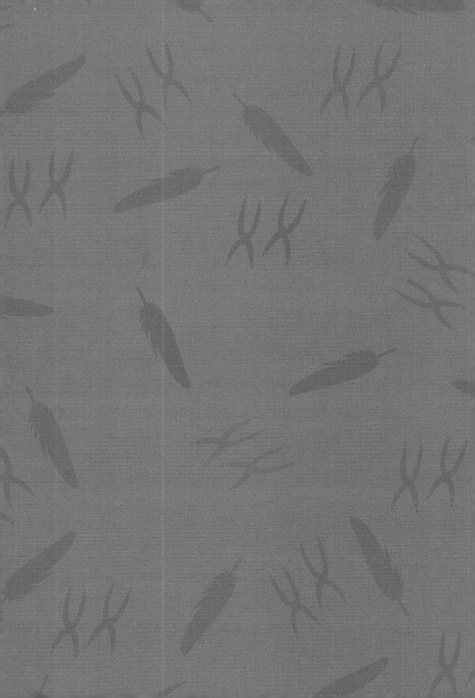

CHAPTER 3

Noisy neighbour

SQUAAAWK! AWWWWK!

I sat up in bed. I had been sleeping, but now I was wide awake. It was seven o'clock. It was the first day of a long weekend break from school.

Ollie was wide awake too. He got off my bed by waddling down his little ramp. I pushed off the covers and hurried to the spare room.

SQUAAAWK!

As soon as Tiki saw me in the doorway, she stopped making a noise. She nodded. Her crested feathers were raised.

Dad came into the room. "She quietened down earlier when I sat in here to work," he said. "But when I left to make breakfast, she got upset."

My dad is a graphic artist. He makes things like adverts and logos. Sometimes he works on projects at home.

"I'll hang out with her," I said. "She'll like that."

I got a blanket and curled up on the sofa bed. Tiki stayed quiet. I slept until Dad called me for breakfast.

At breakfast, Ollie slept under my chair. Mum buttered her toast. I stirred my porridge. Dad sipped his orange juice.

AWWWWK!

We all jumped. Dad spilt juice on his shirt.

"Tiki is very loud, isn't she?" he said, grabbing a couple of napkins.

Yip! Yip! Yip! Ollie ran to the front door. The doorbell rang a few seconds later.

"Who could that be so early?" Mum asked.

All three of us went to answer the door. It was our neighbour, Mrs Sweet.

"Morning, Mrs Sweet," I said. I liked her. She made the best strawberry jam.

"Hello, Kaita," Mrs Sweet said.

"Is everything OK, Viola?" Dad asked her.

"I was going to ask *you* that, Tim," Mrs Sweet said.

"What do you mean?" Mum asked.

AWWWWK!

"That!" Mrs Sweet said loudly over Tiki's squawking. "What is that noise? It sounds like someone is screaming in pain!"

"Oh dear," Mum said. "You can hear that from your house?"

Mrs Sweet nodded. "I'm sure the whole neighbourhood can hear that," she said.

Mum told Mrs Sweet about Tiki. She promised we would do our best to keep Tiki quiet. She also told her that Tiki was a new foster pet. Tiki would be going to a forever home one day soon.

"Well, that's good," Mrs Sweet said. "I'm glad no one's in trouble over here. It's wonderful that you foster pets. But this one is very loud."

After Mrs Sweet left, Mum and Dad looked at each other. They didn't say anything straight away. They just raised their eyebrows and nodded.

Then Dad said, "I'd better go and talk to the other neighbours."

I knew I would have to do everything I could to help keep Tiki quiet. I didn't want her to bother our neighbours. I got my pillow and some books and moved them to the spare room. I laid everything out on the sofa bed.

"Kaita, what are you doing in here?" Mum asked.

"I'm going to stay here with Tiki," I said. "She likes to have someone with her."

"Are you sure you want to spend your long weekend doing that?" Mum asked.

I nodded. I wanted to make sure Tiki was happy. And I didn't want the neighbours to be upset about loud noises.

"I have an idea," Mum said, smiling. "Call Hannah. See if her parents will let her spend the night here. Would you like that?"

"That would be epic!" I said. "Thanks, Mum!"

I always have fun when my best friend comes over. Hannah loves meeting our many foster pets. She was going to love meeting Tiki!

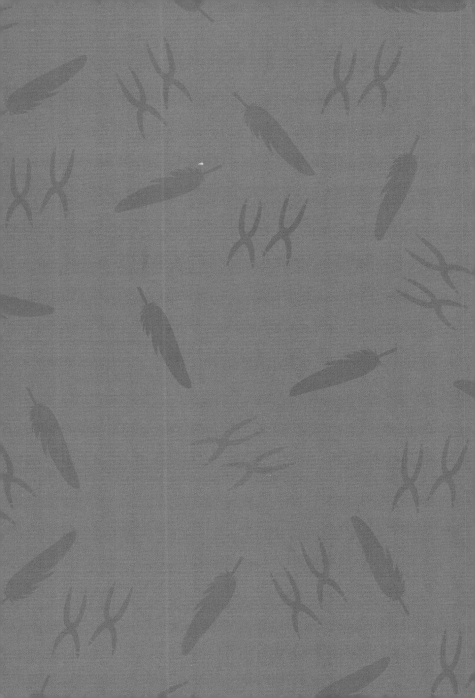

CHAPTER 4

A show for Tiki

Yip! Yip! Yip! Ollie ran to the back door. Hannah was here! Her parents had said she could come for a sleepover.

"I'll be right back," I told Tiki. "Please don't squawk."

Tiki was on top of her cage. She chewed on a wooden toy hanging from her perch.

I ran through the kitchen and opened the back door. Ollie greeted Hannah. Hannah leaned down to cuddle Ollie.

My best friend loves animals just as much as I do. Sometimes, she comes to the pet shop with me to buy Ollie's food. We like to look at the pets for sale. We always wish we could take them all home.

"Thanks for coming over," I said. I picked up Hannah's suitcase.

SQUAAAWK!

Hannah dropped her sleeping bag. Ollie raced into the living room and hid under the couch.

"Was that Tiki?" Hannah asked, her eyes wide.

SQUAAAWK! AWWWWK!

I nodded. It was no use trying to talk over the squawking. Tiki was too loud. I waved to Hannah to follow me. We rushed to the spare room.

As soon as we walked in, Tiki went quiet. But she wasn't on her cage any more. She was on the bookcase.

"Oh no!" I cried. Tiki had chewed the wood on the top shelf.

Dad poked his head through the doorway. "What's wrong?" he asked.

I pointed to Tiki and the shelf.

Dad shook his head and smiled. "I'm not worried about the bookcase, Kaita. It's old," he said. "But not all kinds of wood are OK for parrots to chew on. We have to be careful."

He got Tiki down and moved her back onto her cage. Then he picked up the chewed wood pieces. He used the hoover to get the smaller bits off the floor.

SQUAAAWK! SQUAAAWK!

Tiki seemed to like the sound of the hoover. She squawked and bobbed her head as if she was dancing. Hannah and I held our hands over our ears.

When Dad turned off the hoover, Tiki went quiet again. Hannah and I uncovered our ears.

"Whew," Hannah said. She looked at Tiki and smiled. "You are a very pretty bird, Tiki, but you are also very loud."

I went to the cupboard. We kept Tiki's treats in there. I handed a parrot biscuit to Hannah. "You can give this to Tiki," I said. "She'll love it."

"Here you go, Tiki," Hannah said. She held out the biscuit.

Tiki cocked her head. Then she slowly made her way down from the top of the cage. She hung off the side closest to Hannah and gently took the biscuit with her beak. Then she went into her cage to eat it. She held the treat in one foot while crunching it with her beak.

"Our job is to give Tiki lots of attention," I said. "Doing that keeps her from squawking."

Tiki finished her treat and sat still on her perch. She watched Hannah and me carefully. It was like she was waiting for us to do something.

"I've got an idea," Hannah said. "Let's put on a show for Tiki."

"What kind of show?" I asked.

"One with lots of singing and dancing!" Hannah said.

"Yes!" I said.

I ran to my room to get a couple of costumes. Hannah stayed with Tiki. As long as Tiki wasn't alone for too long, she didn't make any noise.

When I got back, Hannah was already singing. Tiki nodded along to the music. They were so funny!

"Bravo!" I said.

I handed Hannah a costume. She put it on. It was a long, sparkly dress, a necklace, a hat and white gloves.

Next, I put on my costume. It was Dad's old suit, with a purple satin belt. I rolled up the arms and the trouser legs so I wouldn't trip.

"Hello and welcome, Tiki, the cockatoo!" I said in a booming voice. I held a hairbrush up to my mouth and pretended it was a microphone.

Hannah giggled.

"Today, we have a very special show, just for you," I continued. "Here is the world-famous singer Hannah Miller!"

Hannah bowed deeply. "Thank you, Kaita," she said. "I'm so happy to be here. I will now sing my new song, 'Twinkle Tiki'."

Hannah made up a sweet song about Tiki. I danced around the room. Tiki bobbed her head.

After the song, Hannah and I laughed and laughed. We sang some more. We told lots of jokes and made goofy faces. We laughed so much that we almost couldn't breathe!

Mum walked into the room. "Well, it sounds like you two are having a great time in here," she said.

"We are!" Hannah and I said together. We looked at each other and laughed again.

"I think you tired Tiki out," Mum said. "Look."

Tiki's eyes were closed.

Hannah, Mum and I sneaked out of the spare room. We closed the door behind us.

Tiki stayed quiet while we all ate dinner. Afterwards, Mum flipped open the sofa bed in the spare room. Hannah and I laid our sleeping bags side by side on it. Mum said goodnight and turned off the light.

I told Tiki and Hannah a bedtime story in the dark. Then we fell asleep.

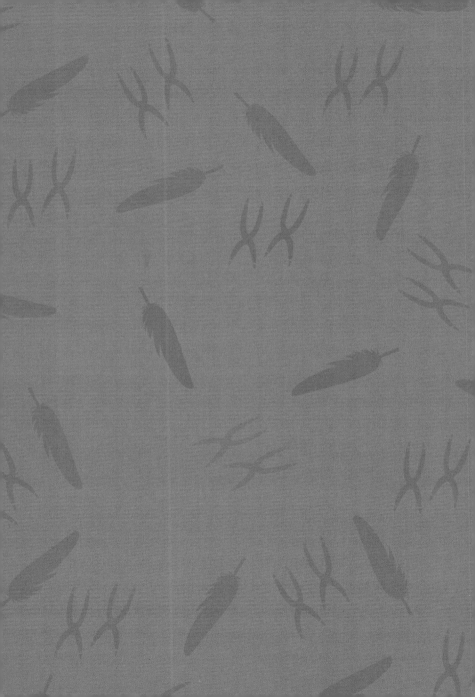

CHAPTER 5

What is so funny?

Ha ha ha ha ha.

The next morning, Hannah nudged me awake. "Kaita, why are you laughing?" she whispered.

Ha ha ha ha ha.

I looked at Hannah. "I'm not laughing," I said. "Are *you* laughing?"

"*I'm* not laughing," Hannah said.

We both sat up and looked at
Tiki. Tiki bobbed her head at us and
laughed.

Ha ha ha ha ha.

She sounded just like Hannah and
I had yesterday!

"Tiki is copying us," I said with
a giggle.

Tiki laughed. Hannah laughed. Then Tiki laughed some more.

Mum poked her head into the room. She smiled. "You two are having a fun sleepover," she said. "What is so funny this morning?"

Hannah and I couldn't stop laughing. Neither could Tiki.

Ha ha ha ha ha. Ha ha ha ha ha.

When Mum heard Tiki, she started laughing too.

"I know cockatoos are good at copying sounds," Mum said. "But this is so funny!"

After a few minutes, we all calmed down. Mum left for her morning run. Dad made breakfast. I showed Hannah how to clean Tiki's cage.

Once Hannah and I had finished eating breakfast, we went back to the spare room. But first I grabbed an empty cardboard egg carton. I got a few pieces of sweet potato too.

Mum had told me about a trick to try with Tiki. She used to do it with her uncle's parrots.

"Watch this, Hannah," I said.

I put the sweet potato pieces into the egg cups inside the carton. Then I closed the lid. I put the carton on top of Tiki's cage.

"We'll see if Tiki can get the treats out," I said.

Tiki cocked her head and looked at the egg carton.

She looked at it for a long, long time. I didn't think the trick was going to work.

Then she climbed off her perch and went over to the carton. She felt it with her beak and tongue. She put her foot on the carton.

RIP! Tiki used her beak to tear open the egg carton.

"Wow!" Hannah said. "She is really strong!"

Tiki quickly ate the sweet potato pieces. Once she was finished, she ripped up the rest of the cardboard.

Hannah and I spent all morning with Tiki. We sang. We danced. We played a game while Tiki ate lunch.

Hannah started looking a little bored. I kind of wanted to do something else too. "Can we go outside and play?" she asked me.

"I don't know," I said. "Tiki will be upset if we leave. I don't want her to start squawking again."

Just then, my mum and dad came into the room. "Girls, we think we have some good news," Mum said.

Could it be? Was Tiki getting a forever home? I wondered.

Dad grinned. "The Parrot Palace has been looking for a family for Tiki for months," he said. "They finally found someone who might be perfect. Her name is Beth."

"Did you tell them how Tiki
screams when she is alone for too
long?" I asked.

"Yes, we did," Mum said. "They knew that already. We told them that you were spending all of your time with Tiki. They said that was wonderful."

I smiled.

"Beth is coming over soon," Dad said. "I need to set up a ramp to our front door. Beth uses a wheelchair."

"Let's move Tiki's cage into the living room," I said. "That will make it easier for Beth to meet Tiki."

"Good idea, Kaita," Mum said. "I'll help you and Hannah."

After we moved the cage, Hannah went back home. Dad took Ollie to the dog park.

Beth arrived a few minutes later. Her wheelchair had a motor in it. It hummed up the ramp and into our house.

"It's so nice to meet you, Beth," Mum said.

"Likewise," Beth said. "Thank you for allowing me to see Tiki." She shook Mum's hand and smiled at me. Then she spotted the cage. "Is this her? Wow, she's a beauty!"

Mum opened the cage door. Tiki bobbed her head.

"I saw a picture of her from months ago, when she first got to the Parrot Palace," Beth said. "She had a rough time for a while, didn't she?"

Mum nodded. "Yes, she did," Mum said. "Thank goodness for rescue places like the Parrot Palace."

"And thank goodness for foster families like yours!" Beth said. "Pets like Tiki need lots of time and love."

Beth slowly reached inside the cage. Tiki stepped onto her arm.

"Hello, you sweet thing," Beth said to Tiki. She turned to Mum and me. "I have two parrots at home. They will love Tiki."

"That's great!" I said. "Maybe your birds will keep Tiki from feeling lonely."

"The Parrot Palace told me Tiki is loud," Beth said.

I started to worry. Maybe Beth didn't want a loud bird. Maybe she wouldn't want to take Tiki home with her. "Do you have neighbours?" I asked. "Close ones?"

"I live in an old farmhouse," Beth said. "I have a lot of space around me. I'm a writer, and I work from home. Tiki will be in good company with me and the parrots."

"You're a writer?" I asked. "I love to read!"

"Yes, I write true-life stories about animals," Beth said.

"Maybe one day I can be a writer *and* a vet," I said. "That would be the best thing ever!" I giggled thinking about it. Then Tiki did too.

Hee hee hee hee hee.

Our squawking bird had become a laughing bird. What a great sound! Tiki was happy. And I was happy she had found her forever home!

Think about it!

1. Tiki is very loud when she's lonely. What are some things Kaita does to keep Tiki from squawking?
2. Joss tells Kaita to handle Tiki only when Kaita's with her parents. Why do you think it's important for Kaita to follow that rule?
3. Tiki laughs like Hannah and Kaita. Why do you think Tiki does that?

Draw it! Write it!

1. Cockatoos need big cages. Draw a cage for Tiki with lots of perches and things to play with. Don't forget her food and water dishes!
2. Hannah makes up a song for Tiki. Write your own song for Tiki. To help you start, try writing new words for "Twinkle, Twinkle, Little Star".

Glossary

adopt   take and raise as one's own

carrier   box or bag that carries or holds something

crest   group of longer feathers on a bird's head

dachshund   type of dog with a long body and short legs

foster   give care and a safe home for a short time

perch   support, such as a stick or peg, on which a bird rests

screech   loud, harsh cry

squawk   make a loud, harsh cry

vet   person trained to take care of the health of animals

whine   long, high-sounding cry

Kaita's fostering tales

Kaita Takano is a fictional character. She is not a real person. However, she is based on a real girl who fosters animals with her family - a real-life Kaita! Real Kaita fosters pets just like Story Kaita. She also has a miniature dachshund called Ollie!

Author Debbi Michiko Florence asked Real Kaita to share some of her family's fostering stories. Although Real Kaita hasn't fostered a bird like Tiki yet, she has helped lots of cats!

Ollie

Real-Life Kaita

K: I think it's funny that everyone always wants a kitten. Kittens have a lot of energy! Adult cats, on the other hand, are super-chilled. Once, we had two kittens who liked to attack everything - and I mean everything. They even attacked a bag of icing sugar and dragged it through the house. What a mess! Adult cats like to nap and get scratched. That's it. Easy. Our cat Meatball was an adult when he came to live with us. He sometimes has a shower with us! He's a weird cat.

DMF: How does Ollie get along with the kittens you foster?

K: Ollie loves kittens! Whenever we get a new litter to foster, he checks them out straight away. Sometimes he forgets he is bigger than they are. He doesn't understand why they might be scared of him. He's not used to being the biggest! After all, he's a miniature dachshund. But once the kittens get used to him, they like to use him as a squishy pillow.

Eraser

DMF: Kaita, you've fostered cats, dogs and even a pony! What would you like to share with readers about fostering animals?

K: Fostering is a great way to meet your new forever friend! You get a first look at the animals' personalities in your home and see how they behave with your own pets. You have some time to decide if you want to keep them or try to get them adopted. Sometimes it's hard to let the animals go. As much as you love them, though, you might not be the best fit. So you just foster them until the right family comes along. When pets find their forever people, it's the best feeling in the world!

About the author

Debbi Michiko Florence writes books for children
in her writing studio, The Word Nest. She is an
animal lover with a degree in zoology and has
worked at a pet shop, the Humane Society, a raptor
rehabilitation centre and a zoo. She is the author
of two chapter book series: Jasmine Toguchi and
Dorothy & Toto. Debbi lives in Connecticut, USA,
with her husband, a rescue dog, a rabbit and
two ducks.

About the illustrator

Melanie Demmer is an illustrator and designer living in Los Angeles, USA. She graduated with a BFA in illustration from the College for Creative Studies in Detroit and has been creating artwork for various clothing, animation and publishing projects ever since. When she isn't making art, Melanie enjoys writing, spending time in the great outdoors, iced tea, scary films and having naps with her cat, Pepper.

Go on all the fun, furry foster adventures!

Apple and Annie, the Hamster Duo

Betty the Bearded Dragon

Buttons the Kitten

Kingston the Great Dane

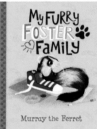

Murray the Ferret

Roo the Rabbit

Tiki the Cockatoo

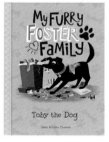

Toby the Dog

Only from Raintree!